JOSH

River Valley Lawmen Series

Book Three

CHERYL WRIGHT

Contents:

JOSH

RIVER VALLEY LAWMEN SERIES
Book Three

Copyright ©2018 by Cheryl Wright

Cover Artist: <u>Black Widow Books</u>

Thanks

Thanks to my very dear friends (and authors), Margaret Tanner and Susan Horsnell for their enduring encouragement and friendship.

Thanks also to Alan, my husband of over 45 years, who has been a relentless supporter of my writing for many years.

And last, but by no means least, thank you to all my wonderful readers who encourage me to continue writing these stories. It is such a joy to me knowing so many of you enjoy reading my stories. I love writing them as much as you love reading them.

CHAPTER ONE

Deputy Josh Wrangler had been on the mountain since dawn, much the same as everyone else.

He tightened his grip on his horse, Brandie, and headed back to base. Not that he thought it would achieve much. They'd looked high and low, and still hadn't found any sign of Laney Jacobson.

He pulled Brandie to an abrupt stop as he noticed the number of volunteers now at the top of the mountain.

Everyone was beyond concerned for Laney Jacobson, as it had been over forty-eight hours since she'd been reported missing, and there was still no sign of her.

If they didn't find her soon, Josh was afraid it would be a body retrieval exercise.

He shuddered. He couldn't bear the thought.

As he approached base, he overheard one of the volunteers. "We've searched high and low, and still she's nowhere to be seen."

Josh's head snapped up. *What if she's not where she can be seen?*

His heart began to race. This was not something he'd thought of before. He kicked himself mentally. Why hadn't it occurred to him?

There were several tiny cottages hidden in and around the mountain. Some were holiday cottages, but most were old worker's huts that were now abandoned.

They were all hidden deep in the forest, obscured by the dense foliage. That was their attraction, and the reason tourists paid big money to stay in some of those run-down shacks.

Josh had grown up in this area and had spent time hiding in many of them as a young boy. As a result, he knew where each and every one of those dwellings were.

Laney's sister, Emily Jacobson, dashed toward him.

Her pretty face was tear-streaked. It broke his heart to see her so upset. He was determined to find Laney today, because if they didn't...

He shook himself. *He was not going to think like that!*

He slowly approached Emily and dismounted his horse, holding the reins as he spoke to her. Despair was clearly etched on her face. Her lips trembled and a solitary tear slipped out of her eye and trickled down her cheek.

"You've no doubt answered these questions before," he said. "But can you help me out?"

He waited for her to respond. She took a deep shuddering breath and nodded her head, her gaze never leaving his face.

"Did she often hike up here," he asked.

She brushed the tears from her face. "No, this was the first time," Emily said. "We only moved into the area recently. Laney loves hiking and decided to check it out. It was only meant to be a three-hour round trip." She finished on a sob and brushed fresh tears from her face.

Josh wanted to pull her into his arms and comfort her, tell her it would all be okay. But that wouldn't be professional, and he didn't want to give her any false hope. He had a bad feeling about this.

Anything could have happened up here in this rugged terrain. She might have come across a rattler, fallen down a cliff, or any other number of unimaginable things.

Without giving it another thought, shocking even himself, he wrapped his arms around her, then gazed into Emily's face as her arms went up around him. "Don't give up hope," he said quietly. "We still have some areas to check out." He smiled at her, as he'd done many times before over these past days.

But his smile wasn't genuine. He only hoped she didn't notice. Laney was in grave danger. With that thought overtaking his mind, he pushed Emily away, and suddenly felt bereft.

He put his hand to her shoulder and felt better. She reached up and covered it with hers. It felt nice, and he lingered, until it dawned on him he mustn't. He'd just crossed the line between friendship and professional.

At that moment, Sheriff Chase Callahan walked over to the pair. "Why don't you go home, Miss Jacobson, and leave it to us?"

Although Josh had only known Emily a number of days, he could tell she was a strong woman, but she'd been pushed almost to the limit by her sister's disappearance.

She straightened her back and stared directly into the sheriff's face. "That is not going to happen," she told him, resolve in her voice.

Chase nodded and began to walk away. "Sheriff," Josh called after him. "Do you have a moment?"

He joined the sheriff, then they huddled as Josh relayed his idea.

"Drury, Marshall, Holden," the sheriff instructed. "You're with Wrangler."

~~~

The four officers sat atop their mounts, hats on their heads, and their uniforms covered by oilskin coats. They needed them to protect themselves
~~~

against the cold and the drizzling rain they would endure deep in the forest.

At each hut, two officers dismounted and went inside while the other two waited on guard outside.

A few hours later and Josh was beginning to feel more than a little disheartened. They'd checked nearly every hut on the mountain and found nothing.

The only mainstay was the fact there were more huts to yet to be checked.

As they approached the last hut, the one furthermost away from civilization, they heard a man's voice. Josh was on high alert. This was not a residential hut. And as far as he could recall, it wasn't even a holiday unit. It was a disused worker's hut; abandoned many years ago.

He was certain of it. It was now more than one hundred years old, and not fit for habitation.

The hair stood up on the back of his neck as they moved in slowly, prepared for anything.

"Good morning," he said to the scruffy looking man sitting on the porch sipping from a mug.

He glanced at the young woman slumped on the other side of the porch looking scared and wary.

The man glared at him and gave the impression he wasn't interested in anything they had to say.

"Mornin," he said gruffly and obviously reluctantly, after taking another mouthful.

"A young woman has got herself lost out here somewhere," Josh said, his eyes darting across to the woman on the porch. "I don't suppose you or *your wife* have seen her?"

"Nope, not seen no one," the unshaven man replied. "Never see no one up here."

Josh briefly stared across at the young woman who gazed meekly into her lap and didn't say a word. She looked too afraid to say anything, and instinctively he knew why.

There was absolutely no doubt in this mind this was Laney. This woman's features were too similar to Emily's, plus he'd studied her photo back at base. Her image was etched into his mind.

He didn't need to see her mouth 'help me' as she glanced up briefly. He was ready to take action – confirmation or not – he was so convinced it was her.

He wore his oilskin coat over his uniform and was convinced the man sitting before them would be even more twitchy if he realized he had four officers of the law standing in front of him.

"Well thank you for your help, Sir. If you do see her, be sure to let the local police know."

Josh tipped his hat to the woman. "You too, Ma'am," he said. It broke his heart to see the despair on her face, but she would surely forgive him in a few moment's time.

He turned to his fellow officers and nodded. Almost in unison, four rifles were pulled from their scabbards, quickly cocked, and pointed toward the man Josh now despised.

As he sat on top of his horse feeling mighty happy, Josh finally remembered to bark out the words. "Police! Don't move!" He wasn't at all surprised when the man sat glued to his seat, his mug suspended in mid air.

Apart from the quiet sobbing of Laney Jacobson, you could have heard a pin drop.

~~~

Emily paced and wrung her hands as she waited at the base camp.

Josh could only imagine how impatient she must have been feeling, knowing her sister had been found, but hadn't been able to lay eyes on her until now.

He helped Laney from the police vehicle, and the two women raced toward each other.

It had been quite an eventful day. Adrenalin was still coursing through his veins, and his heart was pounding in his chest.

Without meaning for it to happen, he'd become very attached to this case. To these women.

If he was truthful, he'd become attached to Emily.

He stared, arms across his chest, as the women stood clutching each other, tears streaming down their faces. If he hadn't remembered the old worker's huts, who knows what might have happened to the missing woman.

To Laney Jacobson.
~~~

He tried not to attach a name to the person, because that way it isn't personal. And when it's not personal, you can't get attached. You can't get involved.

But this time it was far too late.

Each day he'd spent time with Emily, talking to her about her sister, about where she might have gone, her experience with bush-walking, and how long she was likely to survive on the mountain alone.

He'd come to enjoy their time together, albeit shorter than he would have liked.

Josh mentally slapped himself. He couldn't get involved with a victim; it wasn't ethical.

He felt her arms go up around him before he heard her. "Thank you," she sniffed. "Thank you so much. I'll never be able to repay you for all you've done."

Emily's tear-streaked face was against his chest, and he felt it getting wetter the longer she cried. He wasn't used to crying women.

Truth was, he wasn't that used to women. He'd known heartbreak, so these days he kept his distance.

And intended to continue to keep his distance.

He stared down into her face. "You're very welcome," he said, and without his consent, his wretched arms went up around her back.

His hands also had a mind of their own and began to comfort her by rubbing circles over her back. Emily's arms tightened in response.

It felt nice, standing here like this. Holding her close. Comforting this woman he'd come to know and like over the past days.

He looked down into her big brown tear-filled eyes. As a tear trickled down her face, he wiped it away with his thumb.

"Everything is alright now," he said softly. "That mongrel is going to jail," he said, then regretted cussing in front of a lady.

She stared up at him, eyes wide. "I apologize for my language, Ma'am," he said quickly, as he studied her soulful eyes.

She opened her mouth and laughed for the first time since he'd met her. He enjoyed the tinkling sound that came out and smiled.

"I," He knew he shouldn't be standing there like this but was enjoying the moment. He looked up and the sheriff was motioning to him. "Sorry, I have to go," he said, touching his fingers to her moistened cheek.

He stood briefly as he watched her walk to the ambulance where Laney was being checked for any injuries.

The thought of never seeing Emily again broke his heart.

~~~

Brandie trotted over to the fence of the big open paddock behind the Sheriff's Office when she saw Emily standing there. Her tail was relaxed but
~~~

swishing, and Emily immediately knew the horse had recognized her from two weeks ago.

She reached into her skirt pocket and pulled out a quarter piece of apple, which was quickly snatched up.

The horse rubbed her head against Emily's as she chewed.

Four horses were in the paddock, and the other three looked up when they saw Brandie getting the apple treats Emily had brought along.

She smiled, and her hand went up and rubbed up and down Brandie's face. She closed her eyes and drank it all in.

It had been way too long since she'd spent any decent amount of time with a horse.

She heard the other horses gallop toward her, their greed apparent on their faces. She dipped her hand back into her pocket and grabbed out four more pieces. Brandie would want more for sure.

"Hey! You can't be back here!"

She spun around when she heard the deep guttural voice. She would know that voice anywhere. It belonged to the man who had saved her sister from… She didn't want to think about it.

She smiled and waved. "Hey yourself," she said as she continued to feed apple to the horses who were now all lined up along the fence.

He stopped dead in his tracks. "Oh." He rubbed his fingers across his chin. "Hey Emily," he said, striding toward her. "I didn't realize it was you. We don't often get people out back here."

Finally, he came to stand next to her at the fence. "You're pretty popular around here." He pointed at the four horses waiting for more.

She laughed, and he grinned at her. "So, you just happened to have a pocketful of apples?"

Emily had been worried he might be annoyed. She didn't ask permission to visit the horses. She instinctively knew they had to be around here somewhere, so filled her pocket with chunks of apple in anticipation.

She ran her hand down the mane of one of the other horses and rubbed her head against the side of its face. She closed her eyes to get the most out of the experience.

When she opened them, Josh was staring at her. "What?" she said abruptly. It wasn't like she didn't know horses.

Brandie trotted around from behind the other horses and pushed her nose into Emily's hand. "She's greedy," Josh told her. "She always wants more."

His grin lit up his face, and she wanted to see more of it.

Up on the mountain, when they were searching for Laney, he didn't smile. Not even once. His face was lined and tired, and he appeared ready to drop.

But not once did he give in, and she'd known he'd never give up until he'd found her sister. And that's exactly what happened.

Even after he did find her, Josh looked after his horse before himself. She'd watched as he'd been offered and refused refreshments after they'd arrived back with Laney. He waved them away, shaking his head.

He was dog-tired, but refused to rest until his horse was brushed and fed.

A true horseman.

"Are you okay, Emily?" She glanced up to see his face close to hers.

She nodded her head slowly. "Just thinking back to that day up on the mountain."

He frowned at her. "Don't. It won't do you a lick of good to keep going over what happened."

Just then she felt her arm being roughly pushed. "What the...?"

Josh laughed, a big belly laugh. And she loved the sound.

He continued to laugh as he spoke. "You're too slow. They're protesting."

She distributed the remaining apple between the four horses and when she'd run out, took a moment to look him over.

Josh was in uniform today. Although he was that day, the day he didn't want her to think about, but it was covered by his oilskin coat and virtually unseen.

He looked smart in his uniform.

Why did she lie to herself? He looked downright sexy.

"Oh heck," he said, pulling his cowboy hat from his head. "Where are my manners. My apologies, Ma'am. Er, Emily." He seemed downright cross with himself, but if anything, it just added to his sexiness.

He nodded toward the horses. "You look mighty comfortable with them," he said. "You know horses?"

She lowered her head momentarily, then lifted it to meet his eyes. "I've spent a bit of time with them," she said quietly and gave him the best smile she could muster.

She could see the questions on his face. But he was too much of a gentleman to ask, and right now, she didn't feel comfortable telling him her story.

He moved a little closer. Not that she was complaining. It felt nice having him stand so close that she could feel his body warmth.

"I..." He sounded unsure of what he wanted to say. "I have horses on my property," he said. "And Brandie too. She stays with me when I'm not on duty."

She wasn't sure what he was getting at.

"O-kay," she said.

"Would you..."

"Josh, sorry man," the grinning sheriff called from the rear door that only staff used. "I need you if you have a minute."

"Sure thing, Sheriff."

He turned back to Emily. "Sorry, I have to go. But I wondered if you'd like to..." He hesitated again, then seemed to change his mind. "Maybe have a coffee?" He said it quickly, as thought he just had to say it.

She was grinning at him, she knew she was.

She grabbed his hand and scribbled down her number, wondering what he *really* wanted to ask her.

"Uh, maybe," he started again.

She put up her hand to stop him. "Go," she said. "Go to your sheriff. Call me and let me know when."

He nodded, and just like that he was gone.

Chapter Two

Emily sat patiently outside the Sheriff's Office.

She'd arranged to meet Josh here, then they'd go for coffee.

He was late, but he'd warned her it sometimes happened.

She was as nervous as a teenager on her first date. But this wasn't a date. Was it? She really didn't know what it was.

Two people having coffee together?

It had been some weeks since her sister's ordeal, and all Emily had done since then was think about Josh Wrangler.

He was a kind man, she knew he was.

She'd seen the way he treated his horse. When he wasn't riding, he removed the saddle and brushed the horse down, allowing her to rest when he did.

And he'd gone all out for Laney. If it hadn't been for Josh's suggestion they check those old worker's huts, the outcome could have been tragic.

She shivered.

Not because of the cold, but because it was the middle of summer. She put her face to the sun and drank in the warmth. She loved this time of year. Loved being here in River Valley, Montana.

Not that she'd been here long enough to really know what it was like, but because of the ordeal they'd just been through, she knew the people were kind.

Most of the town's folks had been up on that mountain helping to search for her sister. Just thinking about it brought back all the emotions she'd tried to move past, and her eyes filled with tears.

She was quickly brought out of her revelry as Josh shoved the door open and began to walk briskly past her.

At first, he didn't see her sitting there. Then he did a double-take.

"Emily," he said, studying her face. "Are you okay?" He reached over and touched her shoulder, then equally as quickly let his hands drop to his sides.

She nodded her head, and they walked side by side to Aunt Lizzie's Kitchen.

Emily hadn't been there before, but she'd heard about the little café. She was told it was quaint, and very old fashioned, and she wasn't disappointed.

As they entered, the little bell over the door tinkled. It made her smile.

"Aunt Lizzie," Josh said, letting out the breath he'd apparently been holding. An older lady stood up from stacking amazing looking baked goods into a display cabinet. "This is Emily Jacobson. Emily, Aunt Lizzie."

Lizzie was around the cabinet and standing in front of her in a flash. "Oh, my dear girl," she said, grabbing Emily and pulling her into a big bear hug. "You must be so pleased. Our Josh is an amazing deputy." She pushed herself back and looked directly at Josh, daring him to oppose her.

Then she glanced from one to the other and suddenly had the biggest smile. Almost immediately Emily knew what she was up to. Despite being here such a short amount of time, she'd already heard the rumors about Lizzie being a match-maker. "Yes, he is amazing," Emily told Lizzie. "He saved my sister's life."

Her voice broke, and without her permission, a slow tear trickled down her cheek. "My dear girl, you come with me," Lizzie told her, grabbing her hand and dragging her toward a table.

As soon as they sat, Josh reached across the table.

"I'm okay," she said, brushing Josh's hands away. Not that she was averse to having him hold her. Last time he'd held her, hugged her – up on the mountain – it felt so good. She could have stayed in his arms forever.

She'd spent the last few weeks wishing she could be back in his arms again. But on the other hand, he was a cowboy. And she had history with cowboys, none of it good. Emily wondered why she'd even accepted Josh's invitation.

Simple. Because he saved her sister's life.

No, that wasn't true. It was because she liked him. Really liked him.

But he is a cowboy!

She was waring with her own thoughts and it was driving her crazy.

Lizzie put three mugs of coffee on the table and sat down. "You okay now, hun?"

Josh looked from her to Lizzie. As though he though the older woman might put her foot in it. Emily liked her. She was honest and caring.

She hadn't come across that for a very long time.

She nodded her head, then sipped her coffee.

"What do you do, Emily," Lizzie said, watching her over the top of her mug.

Emily could see Josh getting annoyed at the intrusion, but from what she'd heard, this was typical Lizzie. Insinuating herself into her customers lives. Treating everyone like family.

"Right now?" she said. "I'm taking a break. I haven't decided what I'll do here in River Valley, but I have a couple of ideas in the fire."

Lizzie looked at her enquiringly.

"Okay," she said, laughing. Seeing she'd piqued Lizzie's curiosity more than a little. "One of those ideas is to open a gallery."

She watched as Lizzie's eyes went suddenly wide. "Ooooh," she said. "An artist! What do you paint?"

"Mostly landscapes. But I'm not sure I'll be able to make a living from it in River Valley."

"Fair enough," Lizzie said, then let it go. She suddenly pushed her chair back, scraping it along the floor. "I have to get back to work," she said. "It won't be long, and the lunch crowd will be here."

And just like that she was left alone with Josh.

The moment the older woman was gone, she caught Josh staring at her. When he saw he'd been caught, he picked up his coffee and pretended to drink.

Her body was reacting without her authority, and without warning her hand slid slowly across the table to cover his, but she suddenly pulled it away. She had to remember Josh is a cowboy. Okay, he's a cop, but he's a cowboy cop.

And cowboys had not been kind to her in the past. She looked down into her lap. Why was she thinking about that now?

Josh suddenly frowned. "Is everything alright."

"Yeah, sure," she said, knowing it was a lie. "I guess my mind is all over the place today."

He stared into her eyes. "I think we need to start this…. date," he paused after he'd said it, as though wanting her to confirm. When she didn't answer he continue. "Over again."

She nodded, and he continued. He reached his hand across the table and pushed it into hers. She felt a ding of anticipation.

"Hello," he said. "My name is Josh. Deputy Josh Wrangler. Pleased to meet you."

It took Emily a moment to understand what had just happened. Then she smiled. And finally, she laughed. "Hello," she said. "My name is Emily Jacobson. I'm happy to meet you too."

His eyes sparkled, and she could see he was holding back laughter.

Just then the little bell over the door tinkled again. Emily liked the sound of it. Its tone was different to anything she'd heard before. It insinuated so much more than a mere door opening.

<p style="text-align:center">~~~</p>

What just happened?

Josh walked to his car at the back of the Sheriff's Office and shook his head.

He'd made a grave mistake inviting Emily out for coffee. The moment he'd set eyes on her he knew he'd done the wrong thing.

Tessa was in his heart, and always would be.

But Emily was special, and he felt ever so comfortable around her.

What kind of a man was he, to suddenly turn around and invite another woman out? And what was even worse, to enjoy himself.

The lump in his throat wouldn't budge. *What was he thinking?* He sat in his off-road vehicle, his head on the steering wheel.

Emily was nice. He really liked her, but...

"I, I can't do this," he said, his voice cracking.

But he couldn't deny, even to himself, that he wanted to.

As he'd done so many times before, Josh went over that day. Was it something he did that caused it? Could it have been avoided?

He slammed his hand on the steering wheel, venting his frustration. He had no control over the situation, and it annoyed the hell out of him.

What could he have done differently? That question had haunted him since that day, and he was certain it would continue to haunt him for the rest of his life.

He heard a faint tap on the window. "You alright young fella?" It was the sheriff, who just for the record was only a half a dozen years older than Josh.

He leaned back in the driver's seat and looked to his superior. Chase indicated for him to wind the window down.

"Want to talk about it?" Chase was more than his boss, he was a friend as well. A great one at that.

"I had coffee with Emily Jacobson."

Chase studied his face before answering. "Oh."

Josh sat quietly for a few minutes before answering. "Yeah."

"It's been three years," Chase said, frowning. "Tessa would understand."

Josh slammed his hand on the steering wheel again. "Would she? I'm not sure I would in the same situation." The more he talked, the harder it became, and now his voice was breaking. He had no intention of breaking down in front of Chase. Even if they were close.

And Chase had been exactly where he was now, so he knew what Josh was going through.

The sheriff stood staring down at him, his face softening. "If you want to talk, let me know. Day or night."

Josh nodded and started the engine. Chase stepped back and watched him leave.

~~~

"He's a cowboy," Laney said, irritation obvious in her voice. "I thought you'd sworn off cowboys for life."

The look on her face was enough. Laney didn't need to say the words. The moment Emily had told her sister she'd had coffee with Josh, all hell broke loose.

"Seriously, sis, you're over-reacting."

Laney frowned.

"I mean, we just had coffee for goodness sakes!"

Her sister put her hands to her hips. "You promised both me *and yourself* that you'd never date another cowboy." She sighed. "How many cheaters do
~~~

you have to date before you learn you can't trust them?"

Emily stared down into her lap. "Josh is different," she said quietly. "Besides, they couldn't help it if women found them attractive. Especially Chad. He was gorgeous. Model material…"

Laney put her hand up to stop her sister talking, then walked over and sat down next to her. "I know Josh saved my life. And I'm truly grateful." She looked strangely at Emily and maintained eye contact while she spoke. "That does not mean he won't cheat on you. He's a *cowboy,*" she said, emphasizing cowboy to ensure Emily truly understood her point.

"He's not a cowboy. He's a cop." Emily's chin came up and her back straightened. Now she was on the defensive.

Laney stood, ready to leave her sister to her own thoughts. "He's still a cowboy," she said firmly, and left the room.

"I really hope not," Emily said to the empty room.

Chapter Three

Emily stared across at the magnificent scene ahead of her.

She had her paints and easel already set up and had just placed her canvas on the easel when she heard his voice.

"Good morning," Josh said.

His voice sent her heart all a flutter. And he hadn't even touched her.

Paint brush in the air, ready to add her backwash to the canvas, she turned her head toward him. "Morning," she said, smiling.

"You have a gorgeous view here," he pointed to the mountain view the sisters had from their little rented house on the outskirts of River Valley.

"Yes, it's beautiful," she said, continuing to add her watered-down paint. She looked down into the pallet and thought about which color would be her starting point. It was better than gazing at Josh. Every time she did that she lost her cool.

Her thoughts were muddled, and she forgot he was indeed a cowboy. Her sister was totally right – she needed to steer clear of him.

"Would you like to go somewhere?" He moved closer toward her, and she could feel his presence. It was almost overwhelming.

She shook her head. "No, sorry. I need to do this. I'm getting some works together before I decide whether or not to open a gallery."

Emily had begun painting after her mother died when she was fifteen. At the time it had been therapy, and most of the time she'd painted to keep her anxiety levels down. But now she did it because she loved it.

Her step-father had recognized her talent and sent her for lessons. For that she'd always be truly grateful. Now he'd departed this earth, she was pleased she'd made the effort to tell him.

"I've never watched someone paint before," he said, making her more nervous with every step he took closer. "It's amazing. You're amazing," he said, brushing a windblown tendril back off her face.

She stopped painting, her paint brush mid-air. She shivered, and not from the cold. "Josh." Her voice was quiet.

"I could watch you all day," he said, and she was sure he meant it. But she couldn't paint much longer with him staring at her. It was nerve wracking.

She wasn't used to an audience, especially one that sent her emotions into a spiral.

"I need to do this," she said. "Having you here is very distracting."

"Likewise." He leaned in close and kissed her gently on the lips. As he leaned back, she realized she was disappointed. It was the briefest of kisses, almost like an angel's wings fluttering across her lips.

It was light as a feather, but ever so sensuous. She felt a thrill trickle down her spine.

She reached out and touched his cheek, then started laughing. "Ooops, sorry," she said. "I've just painted your face." She didn't feel at all sorry.

"What, like this," he asked, reaching down and covering his fingers with paint then smearing it over her cheek.

"No. More like this," she told him, streaking the paint across his forehead.

They stared at each other for about twenty seconds then burst out laughing.

"I know I shouldn't, but I feel happy when I'm around you, Emily."

She was confused. Why shouldn't he feel happy around her? He wasn't married, she'd found that out, so what was it?

"What's going on, Josh?" she asked, but he ignored the question.

She decided not to pursue it now, instead wiping her hands on the cleaning cloth, then stretching up on her toes, she began to clean the paint off his face. She tried to look away as he gazed into her eyes.

"My turn," he said when she'd finished. He grabbed the cloth and gently rubbed at the paint on Emily's face.

At first, he stood away from her, then as time went on he got ever closer. Her breath hitched in her throat as his face was just a breath away from hers.

"Josh," she warned.

"Emily," he said quietly. Then he leaned into her.

Suddenly he backed away.

Emily frowned. She liked it when he kissed her. Even if he was a cowboy. A cowboy with secrets.

He stood away from her, gazing into her eyes.

His hands went to her cheeks and cupped her face, but still he didn't kiss her. She could see he wanted to, and sure as heck, she wanted him to as well. What was holding him back?

"Josh?" Something was wrong, but she didn't know what.

He didn't answer, just pulled her closer, his arms slowly went up around her back and slid into her hair.

This was where she belonged – in the arms of Josh Wrangler. It was bliss here, and this is where she wanted to stay.

She heard herself quietly groan and he chuckled.

She abruptly pulled back. "It's not funny," she told him, and then pouted like a petulant child.

But his eyes told her he did not see her as a petulant child, but rather a sensual woman. He also looked conflicted, and she had no idea why.

She took a deep breath, then pushed her hands to his chest. She didn't know what his problem was, but he needed to sort himself out before they could be together.

She'd had too many failed relationships and wasn't willing to risk it again. To risk her heart again.

Now he looked confused.

"I don't think the timing is right," she said. "For either of us."

He took both her hands, and looked down at her, sadness in his eyes. "It's complicated," he said, lifting a hand to her cheek.

They had a connection, a real connection. Sparks flew every time they were together, and she was certain she was falling in love with him.

Her heart was breaking, but she wouldn't force him to stay with her. That would never work. For either of them.

"Talk to me Josh," she finally said. "Maybe we can sort it out."

Instead of talking, he slowly backed off, still holding her hands until they dropped away.

"I'm sorry," he said, staring into her eyes. His sadness was evident in his voice. "Goodbye, Emily," he finally said. Then turned and walked away.

She felt as though her heart had shattered into millions of tiny pieces.

<div align="center">~~~</div>

"What happened with that girl of yours?"

Lizzie was onto him the second he walked in the door of Aunt Lizzie's Kitchen. "I heard you broke up."

Josh didn't feel like doing this right now. Actually, he didn't feel like doing it ever.

He hadn't seen Emily for nearly two weeks, and he'd hoped by now everyone would have forgotten. He should have realized Lizzie wouldn't let it go.

She was like a bull at a red rag when she put her mind to it.

"It wasn't working out." He knew it wasn't true, and missed Emily like crazy, but refused to make eye contact, otherwise Lizzie would be onto him.

"Bull."

The older woman came around from behind the counter and confronted him, hands on her hips. "You listen to me, Josh Wrangler. Emily was perfect for you, and you are perfect for her."

She continued to stand in front of him, staring him down. "And you know it."

He looked over her shoulder and into the interior of the shop. At least it was empty, and no one would hear their very personal conversation.

She continued to stare at him and he thought about turning around and walking right back out that door. But he knew he couldn't do it. He would never disrespect Lizzie. And she knew it.

Suddenly her eyes opened wide. "You haven't told her, have you?"

She moved forward and put her arms around him. "My dear boy, get it out in the open." He could hear her voice breaking, and he wasn't sure he could risk speaking for the same reason.

Instead he shook his head.

She let her arms fall to her sides and stepped back and looked him in the eye.

"She doesn't need to know," he said quietly. "We're not together any more."

Lizzie sighed. He could see she was getting exasperated with him, so hopefully she'd give up. But knowing Lizzie that was a no.

"Josh," she said quietly.

He shook his head again, hoping she'd let it go.

"It's important, you have to tell her."

"Not any more," he said. "We broke up, remember." Something he deeply regretted, but it wasn't working out between them.

Another lie.

"Josh," Lizzie said again. "Look at me." He didn't want to, but he was taught to respect his elders and women, and Lizzie was both, so what choice did he have?

"It wasn't your fault," she said, brushing an errant tear from her face.

Damn the woman! Why did she have to do this to him? He was dealing with it.

"So everyone tells me."

She continued to stare at him, not budging from her position right in front of him. "It's wasn't your fault," she said again, this time a little softer.

He glanced over her shoulder again then spoke quietly. "If you say so."

She stepped closer to him, this time reaching out to touch his cheek. "Josh," she said very softly. "It wasn't your fault."

This time they came together in a hug and cried until they were spent.

CHAPTER FOUR

Emily had tried desperately not to think about Josh Wrangler.

But it wasn't working.

Everywhere she went in town, there were signs of him.

Okay, not him specifically, but people he knew, the Sheriff's Office, Aunt Lizzie's Kitchen, and a few other places where she'd seen him over the past few weeks. Including where she lived.

She was smitten at the very least, but he wasn't giving her a chance. He had made the decision to break up. Him alone. She wasn't given any choice in the matter and it annoyed the heck out of her.

Sure, she was a little reluctant in the beginning, but had warmed to him. Josh was not like the other cowboys she'd dated. He didn't try to use her, and while they were together, if you could call it that, he didn't cheat on her.

To be honest, she wasn't certain he'd dated for a very long time. He seemed to be quite raw when it came to women.

She was the total opposite. She was well experienced in the dating game, but just didn't seem to pick the right cowboy. Which is exactly why she'd sworn off cowboys.

She needed to get the fog out of her brain and had hired a horse for the afternoon. It would also be a great way for her to get to know the River Valley area better.

Apart from the odd trip into town to visit the horses behind the Sheriff's Office, she'd mostly stayed at home since she and her sister had arrived.

Her horse for the day was Amy, a beautiful Chestnut with a white star at the top of her face. Emily had already brushed her down, added the saddle blanket and saddle, and was now tightening the cinch.

She couldn't wait to mount her.

Emily hummed as she carried out all the tasks she needed to do before she could finally sit atop the beautiful horse in front of her.

It had been a while, way too long for her liking, since she'd ridden a horse. Today was very special to her.

She'd asked Laney along, but her sister was never into horses like Emily was. Truth be told, what she really didn't like was having to muck out the stables, feed the horses, and do all the mundane stuff as Laney called it, like brushing the horses before and after a ride. Not to mention all the other things that went with it, like oiling the saddles.

Emily was cool with that. It gave her some alone time when she needed it.

She led Amy out of the stable by the reins, looking around to decide where she'd go. She double-checked the saddle as she always did out of habit.

Her heart rate hitched up as she held the saddle horn and put her foot in the stirrup. It *had* been too long, but now, here she was, sitting up on this beautiful mare who was her companion for the afternoon.

She put on her riding helmet, made certain she had her cell phone in her pocket, and they trotted out of the agistment and went on their way to who knew where.

Emily breathed a sigh of relief. She really was atop a horse. She leaned forward and brushed her cheek against Amy's mane, rubbing her hand along the horse's face. She had a pocket full of apple chunks, which would surely be welcomed later.

They started off slowly, giving Emily way too much time to think about Josh. She missed him dearly, and her heart was breaking every day they were apart.

What did she expect? He's a cowboy, and that's what cowboys do, right?

She'd been told there was a cowboy code. One of respecting women and doing the right thing. That certainly sounded like Josh, but…

But then he'd broken up with her for no good reason.

She shook her head, trying to stop the thoughts, then sent Amy into a canter. She headed for the township where she knew public land was available behind the main street for horse riding.

Okay, so she wouldn't see much, but she only wanted to explore the town today.

It took nearly half an hour to get there, then she dismounted to rest her horse. Amy must be thirsty, so Emily led her over to the horse troughs that the shire maintained for the many horses that were still out and about.

The apple chunks went down well too.

She decided to walk for a while, holding tight to Amy's reins, and without realizing she'd even headed in that direction, ended up at the rear of the Sheriff's Office.

It didn't take long before Brandie and the other horses came running across, looking for apple chunks.

She'd only been there a short time when she heard the back door open. She felt his presence and shivered but didn't turn around. Refused to come face to face with him.

Josh made no attempt to come to her.

"Hello Josh," she finally called over her shoulder, forgetting her resolve to ignore him. He stayed where he was. "Nice day," she said, wondering if she was just wasting her time.

"Who's the mare?" The words were stifled but it was a start.

She slowly turned around. He stood stiffly in the doorway and made no attempt to come near her.

She might as well leave.

Putting her helmet back on her head, she grabbed the saddle horn and readied Amy to leave. Suddenly Josh ran toward her, breathless.

He snatched up the reins and grabbed her around the waist, stopping Emily from mounting the horse, his face ashen.

"Josh?" She had no idea what this sudden outburst was about, but she had no intentions of staying when he wasn't prepared to communicate.

He held the reins tighter, preventing her from going anywhere. He stroked the head of the mare and looked across to Brandie, who trotted over to him.

"I have to go," Emily said, yanking at the reins and beginning to worry. "I should get her back to the stables."

He closed his eyes and his face went almost white.

"You're scaring me, Josh. What's going on?"

His fingers tightened around the reins, but she'd managed to free herself from his grip. "Can you climb down please, Emily?"

She tried to yank the reins from his fingers, but he just held tighter. She had no idea what his problem was, but she needed to get back to the stables before they closed for the day.

"Josh." Sheriff Chase Callahan stood at the back door watching the scene play out before him.

Emily watched as Josh turned to face his sheriff, then let the reins slide through his fingers. She took the opportunity to turn, ready to leave.

She saw his shoulders slump as he walked toward his superior. As she moved away, she glanced back over her shoulder and saw him appearing to argue with the sheriff. If she didn't know better, she'd guess it was about her.

<center>~~~</center>

"Sit." The sheriff indicated for Josh to sit opposite him in his office.

He was devastated at the turn of events, at Emily atop a horse, and worse still, one he didn't know. How did he know she wouldn't be thrown?

He could only assume she'd gotten the horse via the only agistment in the area, although Jordon Callahan's wife ran a horse-riding school.

Either way, Emily managed to secure a horse to ride. And it didn't make him happy.

He studied Josh as he squirmed until he was comfortable opposite his desk, then stood and closed the door.

"We talked about this," he said, as he returned to his huge desk by the window. The window that overlooked the paddock where the horses were kept during the day.

The window Chase stared out when he was thinking. And he didn't miss a trick. "What were you thinking?"

Josh sighed. He hadn't been thinking when he went after Emily. He was in too much of a panic. All he could think about was Tessa. And what had happened to her.

Strangely, he never panics. There have only been two times in his life when he panicked – the day Tessa fell from her horse, and today.

There had to be some sort of message there, but his brain wasn't functioning on all fours today. He couldn't concentrate, and there seemed to be a lot of white noise in the background.

He shook his head trying to clear it.

"Did you hear me, Josh?" Chase glared at him. "How long have I been rattling on while you zoned out?"

He stood up, and Josh followed suit. "No matter. I'm obviously not getting through."

"You know how it is," Josh said, expecting some sympathy from Chase. "You've been there."

The sheriff's face went blank. "Yes. Yes, I have," he said. "And we both know it's not fun. But here's the crunch." He sat on the edge of the desk, rubbing his hand across his clean-shaven chin. "If you continue this way, you're going to scare her off. I know you're worried, and I know you can't help it. In every other area of your life you're very disciplined. You're going to have to do the same when it comes to Emily."

Josh glared at his superior.

"Take the rest of the day off and think about what I've said," Chase told him quietly. "Unless you want Emily to turn her back on you forever."

He extended his hand and Josh took it. "This is not punishment, Josh," he clarified. "Take it as a day of contemplation. You and Emily deserve to be happy, but that won't happen if things continue like this."

Josh grabbed his hat and shoved it on his head. "Sure thing, Sheriff," he said flippantly.

Chase frowned at him, looking slightly annoyed. "I'm trying to help you, Josh."

He held the door open for Josh to leave.

"I know," Josh said. "But it's a little hard to swallow right now."

Josh left the building thinking about the only two women who, apart from his mother, had ever mattered in his life.

~~~

Emily's cell rang until finally it went to voice mail.

It had taken all his courage to call her. After what he'd done today, she'd probably never speak to him again.

And he couldn't blame her. Chase was right – he had to tell her the truth. Get it all out in the open. Until that happened, he couldn't see them getting back together.
~~~

And he desperately wanted to get back with Emily. She made him feel things he hadn't felt in a very long time.

He sat back in the lounger on the porch, his eyes closed, taking in the sunshine. The weather was beautiful, and far from what it was the day they'd rescued Emily's sister.

Little did he know what that meeting would bring.

That his life would be forever changed.

His cell buzzed. "Wrangler," he barked down the line. "Oh, sorry Emily," he said more civilly.

He waited while Emily spoke her mind over today's debacle, then apologized. "I really am sorry," he said, and he was. He couldn't help himself. He'd gone into panic mode and the rest just happened.

"So you got home alright?" he asked, wanting to be assured she'd gotten back safely after her ride. Emily wanted him to explain himself. To explain his behavior. She deserved that, at the very least, she said.

"We need to talk," he said quietly, not sure where he would even start. "Somewhere private," he added. What he had to say was personal. He didn't want the whole of River Valley to hear their conversation.

"What about the picnic grounds," he said. "It will be deserted at this time of day." She agreed to meet him there and brushed aside his offer to pick her up. He could understand that. If she didn't like the outcome, she'd want to make her own way home.

They agreed on fifteen minutes from now; the sooner the better, he'd decided. Then quickly ended the call.

He stood and stretched himself out, then took some deep breaths. Josh had no idea how he was going to begin this excruciating conversation.

~~~

He stood at the top of the hill near the picnic table and looked out over the township. It really was a beautiful place.

He'd lived in River Valley most of his adult life, moving there due to a work transfer. When he finished his training, he was stationed in the city, but the lifestyle didn't suit him, and he'd asked for a transfer to somewhere smaller, more intimate.

Somewhere he could get to know the locals. He hated that everyone who came into the city office was a stranger. That there was no connection of any sort.

Sometimes though, he wished for the distance. He wouldn't be feeling the pain he was enduring right now if he'd still been back in the city.

But then again, he'd have never met Tessa. He swallowed hard, then turned as he heard a twig break behind him.

He smiled the moment he set eyes on her. "Emily," he whispered.

She wrapped her arms around herself and looked out across the view. "It's beautiful up here," she
~~~

said, avoiding eye contact with him. "I should bring my paints up here sometime."

"Not alone," he said quickly. "It's not safe to be here alone." The words were out of his mouth before he could stop them. He was too protective for his own good.

She frowned and turned away from him.

"I'm sorry," he said, moving toward her. "I, I just worry about you, is all." He put his hand to her arm, but she shook him away.

Her eyes glared into his. "I'm not your property, Josh," she snapped, then took a few steps away from him. "What did you want to talk about? I can't stay long."

He could see she was angry, and he couldn't blame her. After all, it was all on him. Chase and Lizzie were both right – he should have told her in the beginning.

He should never have left it this long to tell her. "Can we sit down," he asked, already beginning to guide her toward the picnic table, where they sat.

His mouth was suddenly dry, and he wasn't sure how he could even talk. He spotted the drinking fountain and took a few sips. It didn't help much.

"Chase and Lizzie, they,"

She interrupted him, annoyed and frowning. "They what?"

"Never mind, it's all on me. I should have told you from the start," he said, his mouth fully parched this time despite the water he'd already sipped. So much so, he could barely speak.

"Should have told me what?" He could see her curiosity was piqued now, but she was still frowning. Still annoyed.

"That I was to be married..."

She suddenly stood. "You are getting married to someone else? You, you," She stumbled over her words, pure anger over her face. "This is why I don't date cowboys!"

Her fists were tightly closed, and she was visibly shaking. She hadn't let him finish, and now things were threatening to become even worse than before.

He swallowed down the huge lump in his throat.

"You misunderstood," he said as quickly as he could get the words out of his mouth. "Emily," he said almost whispering. "Please – sit down and this time let me finish."

She was still angry, but nodded and sat, no longer looking at him, instead staring across the horizon, watching as the sun began to set.

"I *was* to be married," he said, taking a huge breath before he spoke. "But my fiancée, she, she," he choked back the emotion, not sure how he would get the words out.

She turned her head toward him, sensing something was not right, reaching out and holding his hand.

He took another deep breath and licked his lips. The next words came out in a rush. "She died." The emotion that hit him at that moment threatened to overtake him. Emily squeezed his hand, and when he looked into her eyes, saw tears welling up.

He turned his head away. Her tears were threatening the small hold he had on his own emotions.

"Oh Josh, I can't even begin to imagine what you've been through."

He turned back to her but couldn't speak. He simply nodded.

"What happened," she asked, so quietly he almost didn't hear her.

"It was a riding accident." He swallowed hard. "She fell and hit her head on a rock. She died almost immediately."

He saw the realization cross her face. "Is that... Of course it is. Why didn't you tell me? And I've made things worse for you," she said. "I'm so very sorry I put you through that."

He stood abruptly and stared down at her. "This is not about the other day," he said, then sat down again. "Actually, I guess it is. Because certain people have forced me to look at what I've been doing lately. How I've treated you."

She grinned. "Chase and Lizzie, right?"

"Yep."

She yanked on his hands and pulled him back down to her level.

"I'm really sorry, Josh. I just wish you'd told me sooner. Perhaps things might have been – better. Easier," she said, still holding his hands. "For both of us."

He stared into her face and nodded.

"When?" she asked quietly. "How long ago did it happen?"

His pain was her pain. He could see it all over her face.

He swallowed hard. "Three years ago. But sometimes it feels like it was just yesterday."

Chapter Five

Josh was nervous with anticipation. Emily was coming today.

Oh heck, Emily was coming today!

He ran around the house making sure everything was tidy. Had he washed the dishes? Put his smalls in the laundry? Swept the floor?

He forced himself to take a few calming breaths, sitting on a kitchen chair as he did so.

He counted off the jobs he needed to do on his fingers, and realized he'd done them all. Why was he so darned nervous?

Because this was the first time he'd had a woman to the house since Tessa.

He swallowed the huge lump that had suddenly formed in his throat, and took ten slow, deep breaths.

Looking around, he saw her everywhere. All the little touches, like the picture hanging in the entrance. The cushions on the lounge chair. Even the mat outside the back door where she made him wipe his muddy shoes.

They were all down to her.

He couldn't do it.

He couldn't bring another woman here. To the house they… built together.

It broke his heart all over again.

But he'd promised Emily, and he didn't break promises. Especially to women.

He strode purposely outside and pulled on his dark brown intricately carved cowboy boots. The ones Tessa had bought him for Christmas a few months before he'd lost her.

It pulled him up cold.

Ah heck!

It was never going to change. He would always be surrounded by memories of Tessa. He would always be reminded of her no matter where he looked. Not that he wanted to forget her, because he certainly didn't.

And just like that, out of nowhere, he knew the reason he was feeling like he was. *He felt guilty.*

Not that he had anything to feel guilty for – he'd been told so repeatedly. And Josh even started to believe it, but now that he was bringing another woman to the house, *their house,* things were starting to get a big sticky.

He loved this ranch, the place where they'd been so happy. Where they had made so many plans.

There was a sudden cold draft, and he looked to the sky. The sun was trying to peak through, so he needed to make the most of it. He reached through the back door and grabbed his cowboy hat. Then he was on his way to Emily's house, promising not to think of Tessa again today, if only for Emily's sake.

~~~

Oh my!

His house was beautiful. Inside and out. It was obvious there had been a woman's touch at some point. Tessa's touch no doubt. Or maybe he'd hired an interior decorator?

Emily shook her head. She couldn't see Josh doing something like that.

She stood on the porch staring out across the huge paddock there. Her eyes moved to the right, and she saw the stables.

"How many horses do you have?" she asked, turning her head in his direction. She could see at least one horse way off in the distance and wondered if it was Brandie. She seemed to have an affiliation with her. But perhaps it was just because of the apples?

She'd brought more along with her today. She hoped Josh didn't mind too much. He didn't seem concerned yesterday.

"I have three, including Brandie," he told her, as he moved closer. He stood not far behind her. Close
~~~

enough that she knew he was there, but not close enough to touch.

She longed to touch him. But she vowed not to. Not after he'd opened up his soul to her.

She spun around to ask him something and found herself seriously close to his face. They stared into each other's eyes for what seemed a lifetime. His eyes reminded her of sapphires, and she couldn't pull her gaze away.

She continued to stare, and saw sadness, but he suddenly wrenched his gaze away. As though he had something to hide. But he didn't. Not anymore – it was all out in the open now.

For a brief moment she wondered what he'd seen when he looked into her eyes, but more than that, she wondered about his state of mind. With all those reminders of Tessa around him all the time.

"Emily? Are you okay," he asked, staring at her. He moved closer, until their bodies touched. That brought her out of her revelry. "Emily?"

She blinked a few times, then spoke. "Yeah, sure. Sorry. Just in a world of my own."

She took a deep breath and turned back toward the paddock, watching as the horses galloped toward them.

"I'm willing to bet you have apples in those deep pockets of yours," he said as he laughed.

"Sure have."

He took her hand and led her to the paddock fence. It felt warm and comfortable. And natural. As though they'd done it a million times before, and this wasn't the first time.

She looked down at their entwined hands and he immediately let go. "Oh no," she protested, despite knowing the more they touched, the closer she felt to him. "I didn't mean..."

"I'm really sorry," he said, as though he'd done something that was going to harm her.

Without thinking, she reached down and put her hand back in his. "I like it," she said, and she did. He smiled tentatively.

"I, er..." He hesitated, and she knew there was something he hadn't told her. Something he needed to get off his chest.

"It's been a long time," he finally said in a rush. Suddenly letting out a whoosh of breath. "Tessa and I, we built this house together. I haven't brought anyone here since she..."

He didn't finish the sentence, but she knew exactly what he meant.

"It's okay," she said, grimly. "It's been a long time for me too." They could comfort each other, and each help heal the other?

But that was stupid.

It wasn't like they knew each other. *Really* knew each other.

Her breath hitched in her throat.

She hoped that would change. Emily had no idea what it was about Josh, especially with him being a cowboy and all, but she felt incredibly comfortable in his company.

He squeezed her hand and they moved closer to the fence. The first to arrive was Brandie, pushing at Emily's hand to try and coerce her into giving her some apple.

After Brandie, Evie arrived – a beautiful chestnut with a white blaze down her face. Last of all came Tobie, a young Dapple Gray with a big personality.

They took turns with taking apple, although clearly, they weren't happy about it.

"Would you like to see the stables?" He suddenly changed the subject.

It had been on her mind, but she didn't want to ask. She couldn't help it, she liked to see how people had their stables set up.

They hadn't been there long when Brandie trotted in too. Emily laughed. "Does she always do this?" she asked, quite taken aback.

"Yeah. That's her way of telling me to brush her." He reached over and grabbed a soft brush and began to brush the lackadaisical horse. Brandie rubbed her head against Josh's shoulder as if in thanks.

Her tail remained relaxed for a few minutes, but she then began swishing it back and forth. "That's it," Josh said. "She's had enough. Once that tail starts swishing around, the brush goes back." He laughed at the horse's antics.

"She knows her limits." Brandie's head went down to the pocket of Emily's skirt. "Uh, no, Brandie. You've had enough for now," Emily said, laughing and pushing the horse's head away from temptation.

She persisted until finally, Josh slapped her lightly on her rear. She neighed at him, in disgust no doubt, then joined the other horses in the paddock.

~~~

Josh floundered around in the kitchen preparing a salad for lunch.

Emily sat at the small table watching him, since he declined her offer of help. Her eyes followed his every move, which made him even more nervous.

Oh, she'd offered to help, but then they'd be in too close a proximity, and he wasn't sure he could cope with that right at this moment.

"I bought a fresh quiche from Aunt Lizzie's before I picked you up. It's still warm," he said as he continued putting the salad together.

He wasn't the best cook in the world, but he could put together a mean salad. And slice a quiche.

Placing them on the table in front of Emily, he offered her a drink. "Water," she said. "Thanks."

Josh organized her water, along with a few cubes of ice, then sat down opposite her. He mentally slapped himself and groaned.

When he looked up, she was frowning. "I forgot the plates and cutlery," he said getting up again. She smiled, and he knew it was going to be a difficult
~~~

afternoon. Not because of her per se, but because of his nerves. And her smile.

When a single smile sent your hormones swirling, you automatically knew you were a goner.

As he put a plate in front of her, his fingers brushed her hand. A burst of electricity shot up his arm. She looked up quickly, and he wondered if she'd felt it too.

He dished a slice of quiche onto her plate. "Help yourself to the salad," he told her, moving toward his own seat at the table.

"Tell me about this property, Josh," she said. "I mean, it's pretty big for only three horses." She appeared genuinely interested, and he knew he had to tell her.

He winced inside.

Placing his cutlery on the table, Josh wiped his mouth with a napkin.

"I had other plans to begin with," he said. "Tessa and me. We were going to turn this place into a horse farm. I've decided that three horses are enough for now. All things considered."

He lifted his fork again. "Brandie was my first," he began.

She interrupted him. "Brandie is yours? I thought…"

He smiled. "Yeah, everyone thinks she's a police horse. But no, she's mine. I prefer to use a horse I know thoroughly," he said, taking a sip of his iced tea.

"That way there are no surprises when it matters most."

She nodded.

"Evie was next, and we had her for a while before we decided to purchase Tobie." He looked across to her and grinned. "He's a bit wild, that boy. As I'm sure you've seen. But he's slowly getting better."

"He is a bit cheeky, I must admit," Emily told him. But she didn't seem to mind too much.

"Oh," Josh said, suddenly. "I should have invited your sister too." He felt bad, but Emily didn't seem too worried about it.

"Gosh no. I don't need my sister to shadow me everywhere." She laughed, and he felt relieved.

When they'd finished eating, he went to clear the dishes. Their fingers brushed, and he felt that now familiar electricity running up his arm.

He went to walk away, but she touched his hand. "Emily," he warned, his voice hoarse.

She raised her eyebrows and sat there grinning at him. "Yes, Josh?" She acted innocent, but her expression indicated otherwise.

Was he willing to risk his heart again? He'd answered his own question by inviting her here today. This had to be the first step in repairing his heart and putting it back together again.

"I, uh," he shrugged his shoulders, then, not knowing what to say in response, headed toward the sink where he rinsed off the dishes.

He felt her presence behind him the moment she arrived there. But then her hands went up around him.

His back straightened, and his breath hitched. He felt warmth flood his body, and he turned around to face her, hands dripping with water. "Emily," he warned again, his voice barely audible.

He looked down into her chocolate brown eyes and could have sworn he could see into the depths of her heart.

She stared up at him, anticipation written all over her pretty face. She opened her mouth in readiness, and he slowly moved toward her.

Could he do this? Kiss another woman? In the home he and Tessa had shared together?

His heartbeat quickened, and he could hear it rushing through his ears. It was so very long since he'd kissed a woman. Or even held a woman.

Okay, so he'd hugged Emily that day on the mountain, but that wasn't an intimate hug. *Or was it?*

When he thought back, that hug was what started them on this track.

The moment she'd touched him he was gone. Despite spending many hours of the previous few days with her, until she'd hugged him he hadn't felt a connection.

He took a deep breath and admonished himself. He was lying to himself. From the moment they met he'd felt a connection. And it had scared the hell out of him.

He looked down into her face and saw her eyes were closed, her open mouth had begun to close. She'd given up on him. He had to do something before it was too late.

His hand went quickly up to cup her cheek, and he moved ever so close to her lips.

He heard her groan as his lips brushed hers ever so lightly.

Then he pulled back and waited. It was her call now.

If he thought his heart rate had reached its peak, he was wrong. He stood watching her, waiting for her, and his heart continued to gallop along while he did. Just as he was ready to give up, she leaned against him, and her arms went up around his back. He hesitated for about twenty seconds not sure how to proceed, but then wrapped his arms around her, like he never wanted to let her go.

"Emily," he whispered, realizing he had been using one-word syllables for the past few minutes.

"Josh," she whispered back, amusement in her voice.

His hand went up to her face. "I haven't done this for a very long time," he said quietly.

"Me either," she whispered. "We can do this together."

He nodded his head, although she couldn't see him. At that moment he knew they were both hurting and had to heal before they could move forward.

~~~
~~~

It was Emily's second visit to Josh's house, and she sat outside on the porch watching the sun set.

She should have gone home by now, but she was past caring. Laney wouldn't be worried. She knew where Emily was, and knew she was safe.

Josh was inside making coffee, and suggested, no, ordered her to sit on one of the loungers and take it easy while she watched the array of colors cross the sky.

They'd walked around his property for awhile, the mini-tour he'd called it, and she was worn out now. She had thoroughly enjoyed the warmth of the sun on her face, reveled in the short walk they had taken, but more than anything, had enjoyed his company.

As they were leaving for their stroll, Josh had reached inside the back door and grabbed his cowboy hat, putting it on his head as they'd left the house. She hadn't missed his hesitation, or his angst, as he'd looked across to another much smaller hat sitting proudly on the same rack.

She understood why he hadn't been able to bring himself to dispose of it. It was a subtle reminder of all he'd lost.

She walked ahead, pretending she hadn't seen him. That way he wouldn't feel compelled to explain. Not that she needed an explanation. It was as plain as the nose on her face.

"There's not a lot to see," he said as they strolled through an empty paddock. "It's a lot of the same. Just from a different angle."

When he grinned, his whole face lit up. But his resting face was much more severe. It made her wonder how long it was going to take before he was willing to give his heart to her.

As they strolled along the fence line, the three horses followed from a distance, watching their every movement. Finally, they came closer, hoping for more handouts no doubt.

She turned toward them and laughed. "You lot are greedy," she said, still laughing as she did. "There's none left. You ate it all." She pulled her pocket out so they could see, and Toby shoved his nose in as deep as he could. He didn't seem particularly happy as he scampered away.

They soon came to a cozy little pocket on the property. There was a stand of trees with a small stream running through them.

The moment she saw it Emily found herself running toward it. "It's beautiful," she said, near breathless, she was so overwhelmed by the beauty of it all.

"We must have a picnic here one day," she said, then realized he may not want to see her again. She looked across to where he was standing. "Sorry," she said. "I've presumed way too much. You might not..." She didn't want to say the words.

He strolled toward her frowning. "I might not what?"

Josh stood his ground, looking down at her, his hand on her chin. "Want to see me again." She said the words quietly, hoping it wasn't true.

"But I do want to see you again, Emily," he said, his mouth moving toward hers. He stopped mid-way and his eyes locked with hers. "My life is complicated," he said quietly. "But I don't want to lose you." He lifted his hand to her chin and covered her mouth with his.

<p style="text-align:center">~~~</p>

Emily sat staring at the sky wondering what happened.

Josh happened, that's what.

Her sensibility had gone by the wayside. She'd never intended to get involved with anyone, especially someone she'd only met a matter of months ago.

She couldn't begin to justify her behavior. But it wasn't just her – Josh seemed to really like her too. But he'd been holding back.

At least now she understood why.

She'd never fallen for someone so quickly before. Not ever. What on earth was wrong with her? Maybe it was the uniform. Some women were drawn to men in uniforms.

But not her!

She stood when he brought out the mugs of coffee and placed them on a low table. His arm brushed against hers as he turned, and she felt a ding of excitement.

As he leaned closer to her, he stole a soft kiss. She didn't want it to end, and reached up, grabbing him around the neck, prolonging the kiss.

As she stood there kissing the most wonderful man she'd ever met, she wondered where they could go from there.

He'd said his life was complicated. He could have been describing her life.

"Josh," she whispered, as she held him closely. "Let's pretend everything is fine in our lives, and just enjoy the moment." She looked up at him, and he stared at her for a moment with his sparkling blue eyes, then closed them.

What was he thinking about? Tessa? Work? Their relationship?

She had no idea, but she waited patiently for his answer.

When he opened his eyes again, they looked sadder then ever. He was frowning, and his eyes were still half closed. He straightened up and pushed her gently away. "Perhaps this wasn't such a good idea after all," he said, shocking Emily to her core. It was the last thing she expected him to say.

She pulled her arms away and walked toward the fence. All three horses galloped toward her. Evie pushed forward and rubbed her head on Emily's shoulder.

He stood there staring at her. At her and Evie.

Realization suddenly hit her. "Evie was Tessa's horse, right?"

He nodded but didn't speak for almost a minute. "She loved that horse. And Evie loved her. They were perfect for each other." He looked down into his hands, trying to avoid looking her in the eye no doubt.

She stepped back, not wanting to infringe on beloved memories. Her heart breaking for him. "I'd better go," she said, deciding it wasn't going to work after all.

Everywhere he looked, he saw Tessa. Everything *she* did, reminded him of Tessa. She was competing with a ghost, and it hurt.

"I, I'd better go," she said again, her voice sounding confused.

He looked hurt. "Please don't. Tessa wouldn't want this. *I* don't want it either," he said. "But I do want you."

He stepped forward, wrapping his arms around the woman standing before him. "I wanted this to be the start of something special," he said. "Instead I seem to be alienating you."

She leaned her head on his chest and wrapped her arms around his back. "I don't want to go," she said softly. "I also don't want to intrude on your memories. It must be very difficult for you." She reached up and swiped a tear from her face.

She was so confused, Emily wasn't sure if she was crying over his dead fiancée, or the fact she might be breaking up with Josh.

The last thing she wanted to do was break up with him. She'd missed him terribly in those few weeks they were apart. She'd never felt so miserable, or so affected by a man.

All she'd done was think about Josh, and what he might have been doing at any given time.

"I really like you, Josh," she said, looking up at him.

He brushed an errant tear from her face.

"I'm sorry your fiancée died," she told him honestly. "Do you think there's any chance for us?"

He frowned, and she pulled back.

"I mean, I don't want to intrude. If that's not what you want, just say so, and I promise not to contact you again."

He reached out and pulled her closer. "Emily," he said in a whisper. "I'm in love with you. You are far from intruding."

Her heart beat rapidly, and her head spun. *He loved her? Why the heck didn't he tell her instead of putting her through all this angst?*

Her breath hitched in her throat, and she stepped forward, wrapping her arms around him once more. "You are? Then why the heck didn't you say so?" She squeezed him tight, then looked up into his eyes. "I fell in love with you that very first day. The day you began to search for my sister on top of that mountain."

He brushed her cheek with his fingers, and she couldn't stop the flow of tears. Happy tears.

~~~
~~~

Lizzie grinned as they walk into the diner a few days later. Together.

Josh held the door opened for Emily and Lizzie came around to greet them. "I'm so happy for you, my dear," she told Emily, kissing her cheek.

She reached out and squeezed Josh's hand. "And you too," she told Josh, grinning broadly. She stepped forward and hugged him.

He was planted to the spot and held her tightly. "I owe you so much, Lizzie," he whispered in her ear.

She stepped back and slapped him on the arm. "Of course you do, sonny. Aunt Lizzie knows best." She winked and gave him the biggest grin he'd seen for ages, then walked back behind the counter.

"What can I do for you two love-birds?" She shook her head, as though she couldn't believe the news. That they were engaged to be married.

"We'll have two large coffees to go, and a couple of those magnificent blueberry muffins the amazing Charlotte Callahan would have made."

"What? My cooking is not good enough for you," Lizzie asked, joking.

Sheriff Chase Callahan walked in a short time later. "Hello. The gang's all here," he said, a smile on his face.

"Have you heard the news?" Lizzie asked him.

He pushed his hat back further on his head. "The news Josh finally came to his senses? Yes, I've heard that news."

He slapped Josh on the back and waited for his coffee to be ready.

"We're off to the picnic grounds," Josh told him. "Emily is going to do some landscape painting. It should be beautiful up there today."

Chase's eyes opened wide. "Oh, that's right. I totally forgot. When is the exhibition?"

"Two weeks," Emily told him. "I only have a few more pieces to paint, and I'm done." Josh brushed her hair back off her face.

"Her work is amazing," he said. "You really must come to the exhibition."

"I'll definitely be there," Lizzie said. And he knew she would. Lizzie was very community minded.

EPILOGUE

The little chapel in River Valley had gotten quite a work out over the past two or three years.

Lizzie had been pairing up several of the eligible bachelors in the area, and the chapel, being the only one in the area, was getting quite a patronage.

Josh stood at the alter, adjusting his bow tie, Deputy Chris Dolan by his side. "Let me see," Chris said, and wriggled the offending item until it fell into place.

He stopped, hands mid-air as the organ began to play the wedding march, and they both looked toward the entrance of the quaint little chapel.

First through the door was little flower girl Chloe Callahan. She was almost three-years-old, but she did a great job distributing the rose petals along the aisle.

Mind you, she did throw a few handfuls up in the air and try to catch them, but no one cared.

Behind her came Melanie Sawyer, Deputy Jason Sawyer's wife, along with their toddler Lily. She was actively picking up the rose petals and handing them out to the wedding guests, which caused a few giggles.

Emily's sister Laney walked in next, her head held high, so happy for her sister. She swiped at a tear or two as she made her way toward the altar. Josh reached out and squeezed her hand as she took her place on the other side to where the men stood.

And last but not least, Emily stood at the back of the chapel, resplendent in her stunning white wedding dress.

The dress was made of Tulle, with a sequined bodice and an A-line style skirt. Her veil was made of matching Tulle, surrounded by fresh flowers.

Since her parents were both deceased, she'd asked Chase Callahan if he would give her away. He'd been so supportive of Josh, and frankly, from what Josh had told her, if it hadn't been for Chase, today's wedding would not have been taking place.

She swallowed down her nerves and with her arm hooked through Chase's, began the short walk down the tiny chapel. She wished her parents could have been here to share in her joy. She knew they would have loved Josh.

"You're doing fine," Chase whispered in her ear, as though he could read her mind. She nodded, fighting back her emotion.

She looked across and saw Lizzie watching her every move. Watched as Lizzie brushed away a tear or two. Or maybe three. She watched the surprise on Lizzie's face as little Chloe ran over and gave her a handful of rose petals. That made Emily smile. As she turned to the front, she saw her soon-to-be husband, and a thrill ran through her. She loved that man with all her heart and couldn't wait to spend the rest of her life with him.

<div style="text-align:center">~~~</div>

Twelve months later...

Emily screamed loudly, and Josh came running.

He looked to the floor. "Uh oh." He rushed around like a crazy person, and Emily stood back and laughed.

"Are you like this at work?" she wanted to know. "I mean, seriously, you're acting kinda weird."

"No I'm not," he protested, grabbing a mop. She knew it was true.

Emily stood patiently with her hands on her hips. "I think you're forgetting something?"

He just stared at her and ran into the bedroom to get her bag. He grabbed the keys to his 4WD, then took off outside, starting the engine.

She waited in the entrance for him to come back for her, but he never did. Instead he took off down the road.

She was still laughing when he returned a few minutes later.

"Sorry," he said sheepishly, and she wondered how many soon-to-be fathers had done the same thing.

When they arrived at the hospital, they were quickly whisked away to the birthing suite, where she delivered a baby girl several hours later.

Josh had been a tower of strength, guiding her through the exercises they'd learned at the birthing classes, rubbing her back, and letting her squeeze his hands. She'd even said a few choice words now and then.

They'd cried together when their little girl was born.

"I love you so much," he told her.

She was exhausted but said the words back. "I love you too, Josh." Then she was thoughtful. "I'd like to call our baby girl Genevieve. Genevieve Tessa," she said. "If it's not to painful for you, that is." She brought his hand to her lips and kissed it.

He frowned. "I love it," he said. "But you don't have to."

Her eyes were starting to close as she stared up into his face. "I want to do it," she said. "For you. And for Tessa."

Emily's eyes closed, and she was soon fast asleep. Josh gazed down into the face of the tiny baby he'd just been handed and thanked his lucky stars for the day he'd met his beautiful wife.

THE END

Thank you so much for reading my book – I hope you enjoyed it.

I would greatly appreciate you leaving a review on Amazon, even if it is only a one-liner. It helps to have my books more visible on Amazon!

~~~

To see all the books in this series visit here:

https://www.amazon.com/gp/product/B07DYG7SRB

*The **River Valley Lawmen Series** is a spin-off from the popular Callahan Brothers Series.*

To Check Out the Callahan Brothers Series, visit here:

https://www.amazon.com/gp/product/B078W9YCP5? ref=series_rw_dp_labf

All my books can be seen on my Amazon Author Page:

https://www.amazon.com/Cheryl-Wright/e/B0088GDSKM
~~~

About the Author

Multi-published, best selling and award-winning author, Cheryl Wright, former secretary, debt collector, account manager, writing coach, and shopping tour hostess, loves reading.

She writes both contemporary and historical western romance, as well as contemporary romance and romantic suspense.

She lives in Melbourne, Australia, and is married with two adult children and has six grandchildren.

When she's not writing, she can be found in her craft room making greeting cards.

Check out Cheryl's Amazon page - *https://www.amazon.com/Cheryl-Wright/e/B0088GDSKM* for a full list of her other books.